Beamer Learns About Cancer

The Beamer Book Series

Written by Cindy Chambers

With special writing by Gabriella Miller

Illustrated by Jim Huber

First published by Dog Ear Publishing
4010 W. 86th Street, Ste H
Indianapolis, IN 46268
www.dogearpublishing.net

ISBN: 978-1-4575-2246-8

This book is printed on acid-free paper.

Printed in the United States of America

Dedication

...is book is dedicated to Gabriella Miller who is filled with happiness, ...mpassion, strength, kindness, love, forgiveness and everlasting hope. ...e is a beautiful example of all the precious children in the world who ...serve our unconditional love and support along life's journey.

...is book is also dedicated to every child ever impacted by cancer. No ...tter the age, we are all someone's child and all of us need support, ...couragement, and hope and, as Gabriella would say, "A bright, shining ...r to look forward to tomorrow."

WHAT IT'S LIKE TO BE IN THE HOSPITAL

Sometimes you just go to the hospital for a check-up! It's just like going to the doctor's office, except it takes longer, and the doctors might need to do a blood test. To do a blood test, the doctors need to use a needle. It helps if you hold your mom or dad's hand and look away from the needle. But they still listen to your heart, shine a light in your eyes, and take your temperature.

But it's different when you're inpatient. Inpatient means that the doctors say you need to stay in the hospital over night. Sometimes it can be more than one night. You may need intravenus fluids (IVF), which is just salt water that runs through your veins (veins are the blue lines all over your body that help your blood flow) and hydrates you. To put IVF in, you also need to use a needle. Just look away while the doctors put it in. You might be there for another round of chemo (ke·mo). Chemo is the medicine that helps to kill the cancer. You might take chemo at home, or in the hospital. If you have chemo in the hospital, it could take a few days.

Written by Gabriella Miller

Age 10

There will be a person who comes in and asks you if you want anything fun to do. She's called a 'Child Life Specialist'. She'll have movies and books to choose from, games to play, coloring books to color, and maybe even some toys and stuffed animals!

Being at the hospital may seem scary at first, but the doctors are going to make you feel better, and you will go home very soon.

As I always say, 'you may have a bad day today, but there's always a bright, shining star to look forward to tomorrow.' ✪

As soon as Gabriella could hold a crayon she started writing books. Ask her what she wants to be and she will simply say, "I will be an author." Writing for this book is fulfilling a lifelong dream to be a published author. And, this is just the beginning for Gabriella's writing career. Her immediate plans are to write books about (childhood) cancer, with the proceeds going to her Smashing Walnuts Foundation. Smashing Walnuts is a foundation that raises awareness of childhood cancer and raises money for pediatric brain cancer research.

Ellyn Miller, Gabriella's Mom.

Our Special Thanks

To Dr. Rangappa Rajendra for providing compassionate care to so many families impacted by cancer

To Dr. Edward Puccio for his dedication and commitment to excellence in emergency medicine and for his guidance and advice

To Dr. Jill McCabe for her compassionate dedication to pediatric medicine

To Inova Health Foundation for their strong commitment to the community

To Inova Children's Hospital for helping Gabriella and so many other children

To Children's National Medical Center for helping Gabriella and so many other children

To Inova Loudoun Hospital Foundation for their dedication toward helping others

To Gabriella Miller for teaching us so much about kindness and strength and for being such a beautiful writer

To Ellyn Miller for showing us the power and grace of a loving mother

To the Miller family for their strength and determination

To the Rajendra family for helping educate so many children

To Jim Huber for beautifully illustrating this sensitive subject

To Sue, Jay and Serena Huber for their help with this book

To Kyle Mitchell for his kindness toward everyone, especially children

To Christal and Kedric Golston for their kindness and compassion

To Lynn Moffat Winston for her kindness and encouragement

To Debbie and Keith Rieger for their friendship and encouragement

To Sally Pickell for her input, advice and creativity

To Janet Skinner for her input, advice and encouragement

To Patricia, Teresa and Patty for their advice and support

To friends and loved ones who have encouraged us throughout this journey

Hi, I'm Beamer. I'm a therapy dog. I live in a fun place called
Tell Me Town with my best friend Kyle and his family.

I'm going to tell you a story about Kyle, some really cool friends,
and me.

One day, Kyle and I were playing ball outside when our good friend Tayo came running into the backyard looking really happy.

"Hi, Kyle and Beamer," said Tayo. "Look at my hair. It's growing back!"

Kyle and I looked at Tayo and said, "Wow, you're right. Your hair is growing back! It looks cooler than ever."

Right then, I started to remember when Tayo first told us he had cancer and that he might lose his hair for a little while.

Back then, we didn't know what cancer was, so Kyle's mom arranged for us to visit our good friend Dr. Poochio at the Tell Me Town Hospital to get some answers.

When we arrived at the hospital, Dr. Poochio said, "Hi Kyle and Beamer. This is my good friend Dr. Raj. He's a cancer doctor. He's called an oncologist which means he went to school to learn how to help people who have cancer."

Kyle looked surprised and said, "Wow, oncologist, that's a big word. You must be important! "

Dr. Raj laughed and said, "My patients are the ones who are important." Then he shook Kyle's hand and gave me a pat on the head. We could tell, right away, that we were going to like him.

. Raj talked about cancer as we walked down the hall toward his oncology partment. He wanted to show us where he helps people who have cancer.

e said, "When you hear that a person has cancer, it actually means the person as cancer cells."

Then Dr. Raj said, "Our bodies are made up of lots of tiny cells. All of them come together to make us look and function the way we do."

"Wow," said Kyle, looking at his arm, "we're a bunch of cells. I never knew that! That's pretty cool."

Then, Dr. Raj said, "Each cell has something inside of it called a nucleus. The nucleus is in charge of the cell in which it lives. We'll call the nucleus, Mr. Nucleus."

Mr. Nucleus keeps the recipe that was used to create his cell close by at all times. He calls the recipe for his cell, DNA. He's very proud of his DNA recipe. It contains every detail of how his cell looks and functions. He thinks it's perfect!

Then Dr. Raj said, "Mr. Nucleus knows his cell will need to use his DNA recipe to carry out some of his orders."

Then Dr. Raj said, "Here are two examples of orders that Mr. Nucleus might give his cell.

He might tell his cell to make an exact copy of one of its parts. To do that, his cell will want to copy that exact part of his DNA recipe so that the new part will come out just right.

Mr. Nucleus might tell his cell to make a new cell that looks exactly the same as his cell. To do that, his cell will want to copy the entire DNA recipe exactly as it is, leaving nothing out."

"So you see," said Dr. Raj, "when Mr. Nucleus tells his cell what to do, every part of the DNA recipe that is needed, has to be followed exactly. Nothing can be left out."

"It is just like your mom following a recipe to make your favorite cake. She would follow every detail of the recipe, leaving nothing out or the cake would get messed up."

Then Dr. Raj said, "Remember I told you that Mr. Nucleus's DNA recipe contains every detail of how his cell looks and functions?"

"Well," said Dr. Raj, "that's why when Mr. Nucleus gives an order, every detail of the DNA recipe that is needed has to be copied exactly. If anything is left out, the cell will get messed up.

We call a messed up cell 'abnormal'."

Then Dr. Raj said, "There is something else that can happen with Mr. Nucleus's cell. You see, some cells are only needed for a short period of time. Then they have to go away and disappear.

If Mr. Nucleus's cell doesn't go away when it is supposed to, it can also become an abnormal cell."

That's when Kyle and I asked, "What does an abnormal cell have to do with cancer?"

Dr. Raj looked at us very calmly said, "An abnormal cell can become a cancer cell. That's how cancer gets started."

Kyle looked at Dr. Raj and said, "If that's the case, then it's not someone's fault if he or she gets cancer. That also means that a person who has cancer can't give it to anyone else. It happens all by itself."

Dr. Raj smiled and said, "That's exactly right Kyle."

That's when I said, "So that means we can still play with our friend who has cancer and we can still give him hugs. I'm really glad."

Then Kyle asked, "After someone's body makes one cancer cell, what happens?"

Dr. Raj said, "When a cancer cell is created, it is lonely, so its Mr. Nucleus will give the order to copy itself and make another cancer cell. Then the new cancer will do the same and it will continue."

Then Dr. Raj said, "As cancer cells are created, there are lots of different places in a person's body they can decide to show up, and lots of kinds of cancer they can become."

That's when I asked, "How do you find out if a person has cancer, and what do you do to get the cancer cells to go away?"

Dr. Raj said, "Beamer, that's a great question. Tests are done to see if a person has cancer.

If cancer cells are found, the oncologist will decide the best way to try to get rid of them. This is called treating the person."

Then Dr. Raj said, "We know the treatment is working when the cancer cells start to go away."

Then Kyle asked, "Why do some people who get cancer lose their hair?"

Dr. Raj said, "Sometimes the things we use to treat people with cancer cause their hair to fall out for a little while, but it will grow back."

Then Dr. Raj told us that people getting treated for cancer might feel tired, look a little different or act grumpy from the medicine, but that will go away as soon as they are feeling better.

Dr. Raj also said, "Be kind to friends and loved ones who have cancer. Treat them just as you did before they got cancer. Talk to them about the things they like. Let them decide if they want to talk about having cancer."

When we got to the oncology department, we noticed it was bright and colorful with really nice pictures on the walls. There were big comfortable chairs and cool electronics for the kids to use.

Everyone was friendly. We noticed that when Dr. Raj and Dr. Poochio walked in, everyone wanted to talk to them and say how nice it was to see them. Everyone said, "Hi" to us too!

When it was time to go, Dr. Raj said he enjoyed meeting us and he thanked our good friend Dr. Poochio for introducing us. We could tell Dr. Poochio was proud of us for learning about cancer, and happy that we came to visit.

From that day on, Kyle and I had a better understanding of cancer and what we could do to help our friend Tayo.

While he was going through treatment, Kyle and I visited Tayo often. When we did, most of the time we talked about sports, school, and all the other stuff we had always talked about before he got cancer. Other times we just sat quietly and Tayo would pet me.

We let Tayo decide what we would do during our visits.

After I finished thinking about those very special memories, Tayo said, "You know, Kyle and Beamer, I'm glad you spent time with me when I had cancer. It helped me to feel a lot better."

I looked at him and said, "I'm really glad too. You taught us a lot about being real friends, and you'll always be Beamer's Buddy."

Some of Beamer's Real Life Buddies

Dr. Rangappa Rajendra (Dr. Raj)

Dr. Rajendra received his medical degree at St. John's Medical College in Bangalore, India. After completing his internship and residency in New York and Chicago, he did his fellowship in medical oncology and hematology at Washington Hospital Center in Washington, D.C. He has practiced in Loudoun County, Virginia for over two decades. Dr. Rajendra was recently named Medical Director of the Inova Comprehensive Cancer and Research Institute, Inova Loudoun Hospital.

Dr. Rajendra draws inspiration from the amazing children of Sahasra Deepika Foundation for Education (www.sdie.org) in Bangalore, India. Since 1998, Sahasra Deepika has given children who are orphans, or have a single parent who can't afford to educate them, a quality education and a safe, caring environment in which to grow and learn. With the support and encouragement they receive at Sahasra Deepika, the children are given the tools to grow into confident, empowered individuals. The children's courage and smiles in the face of so many challenges motivates Dr. Rajendra to do his best for his patients every day.

Dr. Edward Puccio, MD, FACEP (Dr. Poochio)

Dr. Puccio is the Medical Director for the Emergency Department at Inova Loudoun Hospital in Leesburg, Virginia. Dr. Puccio did his emergency residency at Allegheny General Hospital in Pennsylvania. He did his internship and residency, in General Surgery, at Georgetown University Hospital in Washington D.C. Dr. Puccio graduated from The University of Pittsburgh School of Medicine where he received his MD. He attended Duke University in Durham, North Carolina, where he received a Bachelor of Science Degree in Zoology.

Kyle Mitchell (Kyle)

Kyle is thirteen years old. Along with studying and playing football and lacrosse, Kyle dedicates his time to helping others in need. Kyle is a recipient of the 2012 Excalibur Award from Inova Loudoun Hospital for his commitment to helping those in need, especially children.

Some of Beamer's Real Life Buddies

Gabriella Miller (Gabriella)

Gabriella Miller is a ten year old rising fifth grader. She was diagnosed with an inoperable brain tumor the size of a walnut in November 2012. In the eight months since her diagnosis, Gabriella has become a huge childhood cancer awareness advocate and fund raiser. Through her efforts, she raised $275,000 for the Make A Wish Foundation and $15,000 for the Childhood Brain Tumor Foundation. Gabriella launched the Smashing Walnuts Foundation which advocates childhood cancer awareness and raises money for pediatric brain cancer research.

About Tell Me Town

About The Author

Cindy Chambers was raised in a large family filled with lots of laughter, children and pets. She has enjoyed writing since she was a child. Cindy has been instrumental in raising hundreds of thousands of dollars for charities. Because of her strong interest in education, health, writing, and helping others, she created *The Beamer Book Series*, Tell Me Town Books, and The Tell Me Town Foundation. Cindy has received awards and recognition for her commitment to helping others, and for Tell Me Town and *The Beamer Book Series*. The author and the series have appeared in news and magazine articles, and on television news.

About The Tell Me Town Foundation

The Tell Me Town Foundation, is a 501(c) (3) non-profit, established to provide comfort and education to children and their families as they learn about life, health and safety. Through The Beamer Book Series, Tell Me Town Books, and the Tell Me Town website, children and their families learn about these important topics, in a delightful setting where everyone is treated with kindness and respect.

To Find Out More

To find out more about Tell Me Town and *The Beamer Book Series*, please visit us at www.tellmetown.com, "Like" Tell Me Town on Facebook, and follow us on Twitter.

CPSIA information can be obtained at www.ICGtesting.com
Printed in the USA
BVIW12n1954081116
467274BV00002B/2